The Three Little Kittens

Written by Lee Randall
Illustrated by Michelle Lash-Ruff

©1996 McClanahan Book Company, Inc.
All rights reserved.
Published by McClanahan Book Company, Inc.
23 West 26th Street, New York, NY 10010.
LCC: 96-75640.
Printed in the USA.

The three little kittens,
They lost their mittens,
And they began to cry,
"Oh, Mother dear,
We sadly fear,
Our mittens we have lost!"

"What? Lost your mittens?
You naughty kittens!
Then you shall have no pie."

"Meow, meow, meow, meow,
Meow, meow, meow, meow."

The three little kittens,
They found their mittens,
And they began to cry,

"Oh, Mother dear,
See here, see here,
Our mittens we have found."

"What? Found your mittens?
You good little kittens!
Then you shall have some pie."

"Purr, purr, purr, purr,
Purr, purr, purr, purr."

The three little kittens,
Put on their mittens,
And soon ate up the pie.

"Oh, Mother dear,
We greatly fear,
Our mittens we have soiled."

"What? Soiled your mittens?
You naughty kittens!"
Then they began to sigh,

"Meow, meow, meow, meow,
Meow, meow, meow, meow."

The three little kittens,
They washed their mittens,
And hung them out to dry.

"Oh, Mother dear,
See here, see here,
Our mittens we have washed."

"What? Washed your mittens?
You darling kittens!
Now go outside and play."

"Purr, purr, purr, purr,
Purr, purr, purr, purr."